BEING WENDY

by New York Times Best-Selling Author
Fran Drescher

Teacher

illustrated by Amy Blay

Grosset & Dunlap
An Imprint of Penguin Group (USA) Inc.

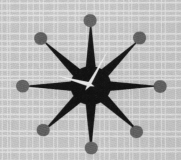

GROSSET & DUNLAP
Published by the Penguin Group
Penguin Group (USA) Inc., 375 Hudson Street, New York, New York 10014, USA
Penguin Group (Canada), 90 Eglinton Avenue East, Suite 700, Toronto, Ontario M4P 2Y3, Canada
(a division of Pearson Penguin Canada Inc.)
Penguin Books Ltd., 80 Strand, London WC2R 0RL, England
Penguin Group Ireland, 25 St. Stephen's Green, Dublin 2, Ireland (a division of Penguin Books Ltd.)
Penguin Group (Australia), 250 Camberwell Road, Camberwell, Victoria 3124, Australia
(a division of Pearson Australia Group Pty. Ltd.)
Penguin Books India Pvt. Ltd., 11 Community Centre, Panchsheel Park, New Delhi—110 017, India
Penguin Group (NZ), 67 Apollo Drive, Rosedale, Auckland, New Zealand
(a division of Pearson New Zealand Ltd.)
Penguin Books (South Africa) (Pty.) Ltd., 24 Sturdee Avenue, Rosebank, Johannesburg 2196, South Africa

Penguin Books Ltd., Registered Offices: 80 Strand, London WC2R 0RL, England

Library of Congress Control Number: 2011003090

ISBN 978-0-448-45688-1   10 9 8 7 6 5 4 3 2 1

To my parents, who always encouraged
my originality and made me feel
I could do anything.

Boxville

FOOD STORE

Toy Shop · Bank · Bakery

Boxville

Boxville
Square

Boxville

Doctors

School

N
W   E
S

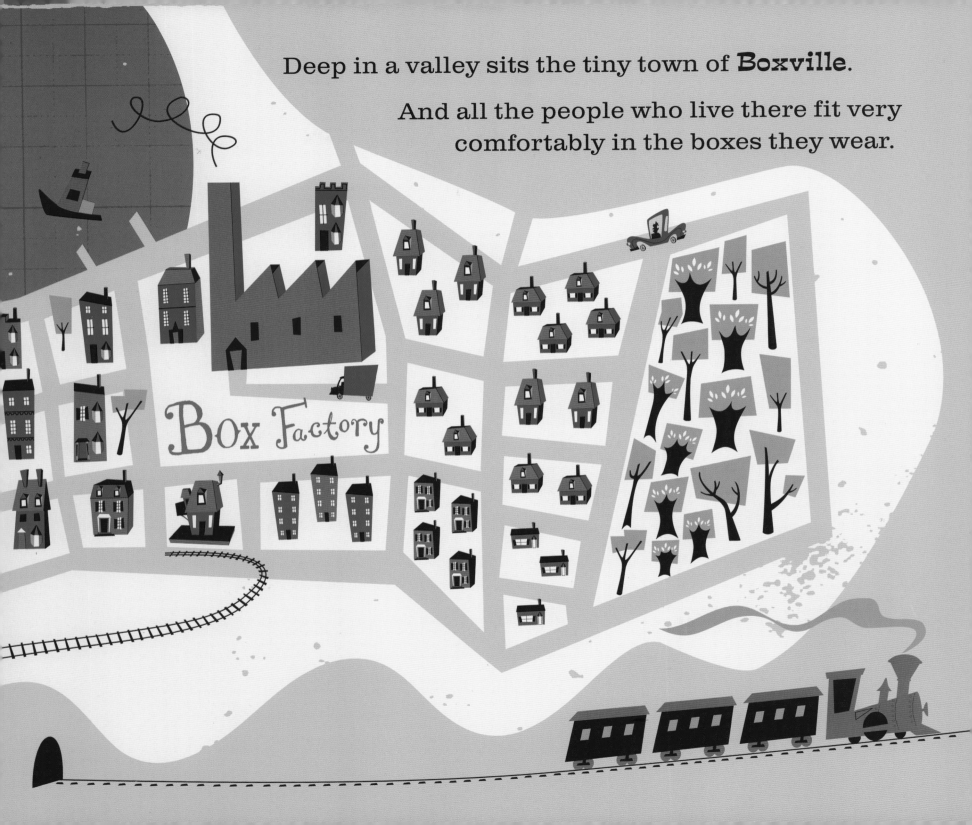

Deep in a valley sits the tiny town of **Boxville**.

And all the people who live there fit very comfortably in the boxes they wear.

Box Factory

As she did every Monday morning,
Wendy Starbright walked to school.
Wendy said hello to Officer Miranda
Wrights, who wore her police officer's
box with pride as she directed traffic.

She smiled at Willie Walkenpoop as he held on tightly to many leashes.

And Wendy stared at the beautiful Bella Fashionista, the dress shop owner, as she unlocked the door of her fancy store.

At school, Wendy's teacher, Mrs. Reedenwright, wrote on the blackboard in perfect penmanship. Wendy looked around the classroom and saw that all the students were happy wearing the boxes they had chosen.

Hope's box said **DOCTOR** because she knew she wanted to cure sick people.

Joe's box said **SOLDIER** because he wanted to protect people.

And **Candy's** box said **BAKER** because she loved sweets.

But Wendy didn't want to be labeled anything at all.
She wiggled in her box. If only she could take it off.

Why did she have to wear this **boring brown box**, anyway?

Wendy was full of ideas. She loved to do lots and lots of things. How could she possibly pick **ONE** to put on her box?

Wendy loved to play her guitar *and* shoot hoops! Should her box say **GUITARIST?** Or maybe **BASKETBALL PLAYER?** Or . . .

Oh, thought Wendy.
How will I ever choose just one box?

She was afraid to say out loud that
she felt different from everyone else.

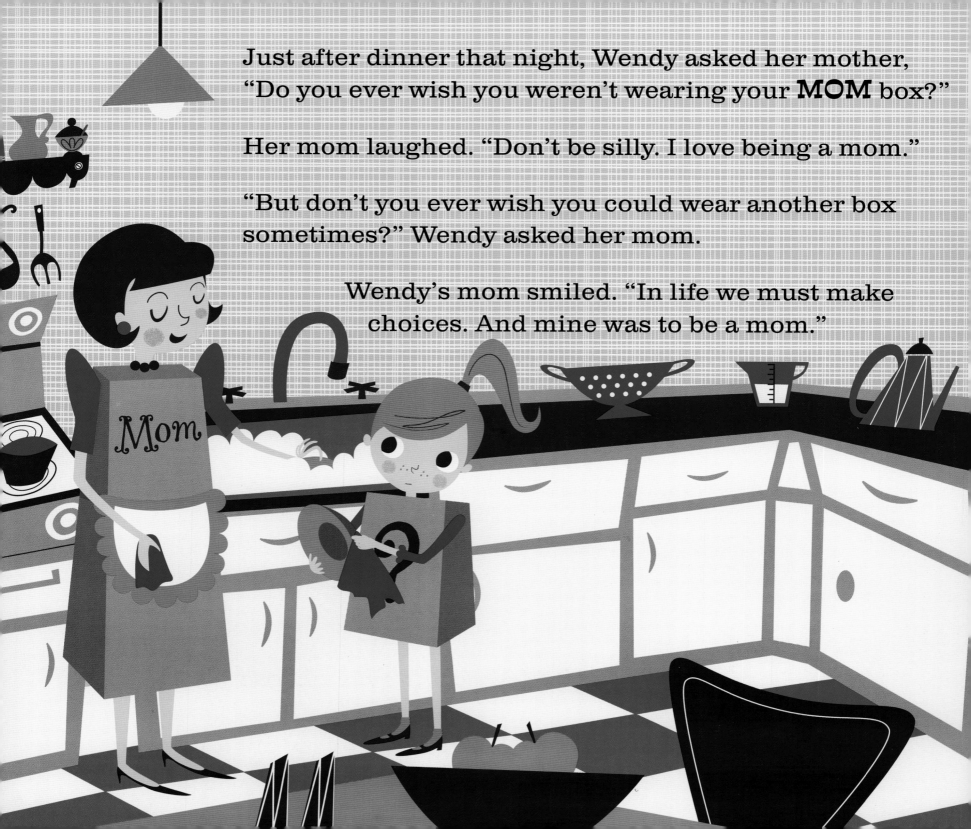

Just after dinner that night, Wendy asked her mother, "Do you ever wish you weren't wearing your **MOM** box?"

Her mom laughed. "Don't be silly. I love being a mom."

"But don't you ever wish you could wear another box sometimes?" Wendy asked her mom.

Wendy's mom smiled. "In life we must make choices. And mine was to be a mom."

Wendy knew she wanted to wear *lots* of different boxes because she had so many interests.

Boxville

She dreamed of traveling the world and seeing exotic sights. **She had BIG plans!**

She imagined herself meeting with foreign leaders, **working for world peace.**

She thought about **running marathons.**

Sometimes, she wanted to be a **great writer**.

Wendy even dreamed of being a **famous actress**.

Actress

How could she do **all** these exciting things if she had to wear just one box? She couldn't.

THE BOXVILLE WAY IS
TO CHOOSE A BOX FOR THE REST OF YOUR DAYS.

The BIGGEST rule in Boxville was she **HAD TO** choose a box and stay in it.

But now Wendy had an idea.

On Wednesday morning, Wendy Starbright
left her house before her parents could see her . . .
without putting on her box!

Out on the street, Wendy caused quite a stir. Officer Miranda Wrights blew her whistle, **but Wendy kept walking.** Willie Walkenpoop's dogs barked and howled, **but Wendy kept walking.** And Bella Fashionista covered her eyes, **but Wendy kept walking.**

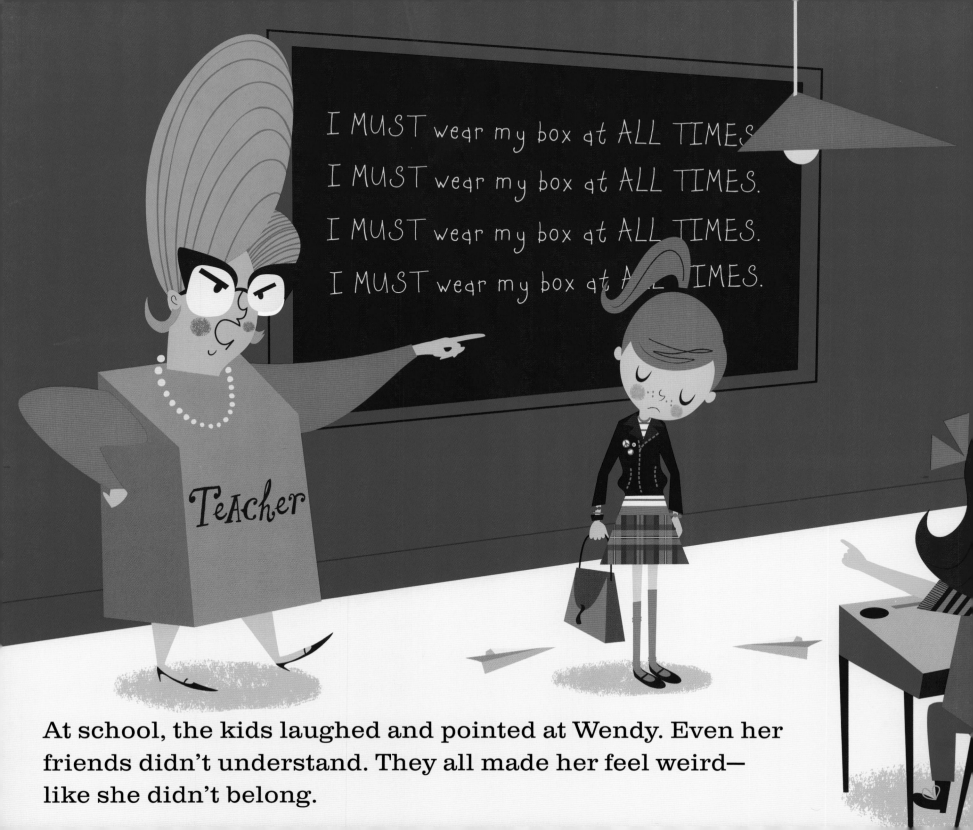

At school, the kids laughed and pointed at Wendy. Even her friends didn't understand. They all made her feel weird— like she didn't belong.

Mrs. Reedenwright sent Wendy to the principal's office for violating the town's biggest rule. "Why can't you just choose a box like everyone else, Wendy?" she said with disappointment.

The principal called Wendy's father. As soon as her
dad arrived, Wendy burst into tears and ran into his
arms. But, as always, his box got in the way.

On the walk home, Wendy told her dad the truth. "I know everyone in Boxville likes wearing their boxes, but I don't."

"You just haven't found the right box yet. But you'll find the one that fits," said Wendy's dad.

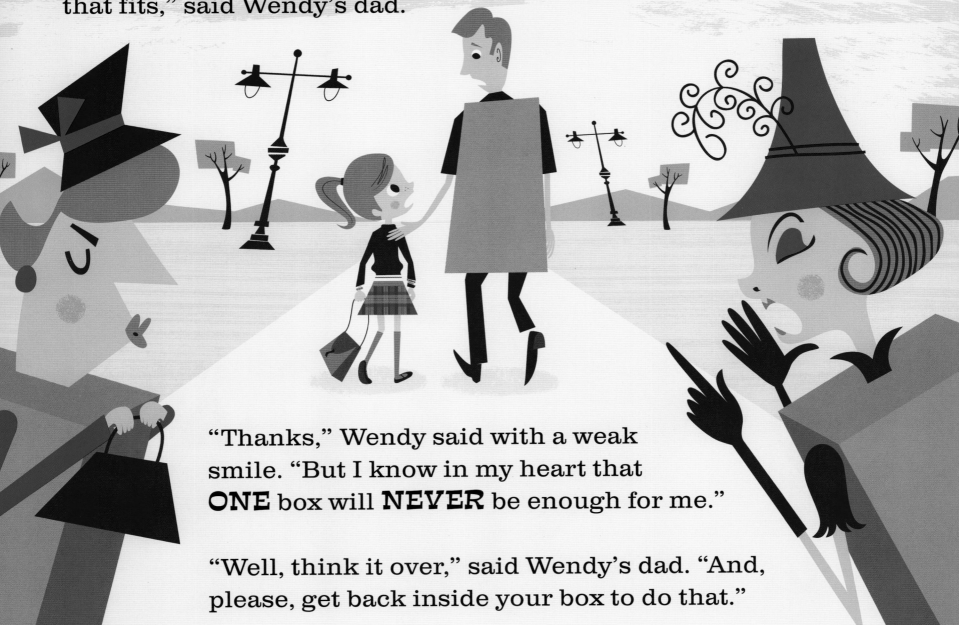

"Thanks," Wendy said with a weak smile. "But I know in my heart that **ONE** box will **NEVER** be enough for me."

"Well, think it over," said Wendy's dad. "And, please, get back inside your box to do that."

Wendy tried to take her dad's advice, but the more she thought about it, the more she hated thinking inside the box. She would never fit in at school, at home, or in Boxville. Being different was lonely. But she couldn't be any other way. **She was different.**

Wendy ripped off her box once more. She took a deep breath and went downstairs to try talking with her parents again.

Her whole family was in the kitchen, but
something was very different about them.
They were out of their boxes!

"What's going on?" Wendy asked.

"Well, we did some thinking, too—and decided that you're right!" said her mom.

"You're a very special girl, Wendy," said her dad. "You have a lot of different talents that make you *you*. And that's a good thing! You should do anything and everything you want. We all should!"

Wendy smiled her biggest smile.

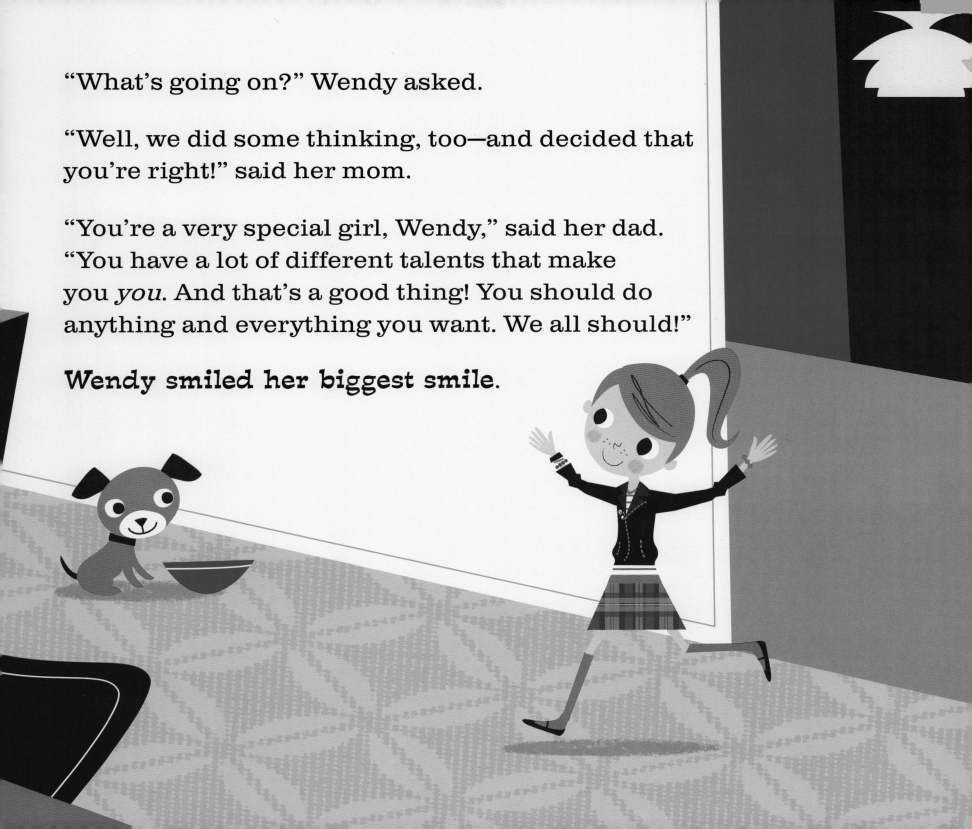

Later that day, the whole Starbright family left the house without their boxes. Wendy happily waved to their Boxville neighbors. She was unique, special, and proud of it.

Soon after, the Starbrights packed their stuff into
their now-empty boxes, loaded up the car, and left
Boxville for a new town called Freedomland.

THE END